MW01170937

2019 "A Roman Soldier Reminisces" by Patsy North

ISBN 9798651555185

For more information on the content of this book, email nanaandus@hotmail.com

JMPinckney Publishing Company, LLC, Goose Creek, SC
Sonja Pinckney Rhodes

Illustration and Design: Michael Jooce Warren

Printed in the United States of America

A Roman Soldier Reminisces

Patsy North

A ROMAN SOLDIER REMINISCES

PROLOGUE:

We would love to think that our past does not define our future - no matter how long it takes. No matter how long it takes, our Lord and Savior Jesus Christ is always willing to forgive us for our sins and mistakes, and He has given us the opportunity to change our lives and be born again. Therefore, we should be willing to forgive others. We all are traveling this road of repentance.

Today is Sunday and Julius, a Roman Soldier, is witnessing another crucifixion of three thieves that occurred on Friday, three days ago. He is now remembering a crucifixion that took place over 20 years earlier. He is broken and downhearted because that crucifixion he played a major role in when he was only 21 or 22 years old.

When Julius was a teenager visiting his friends in the hills of Bethlehem of Judea, about 6 or 7 miles from where Jesus was born, many things were unfolding in his life that he just could not understand. Today Julius has a story that has been stored inside of him for years and now he has a need to talk about it with someone after witnessing this crucifixion of the three thieves. Can he talk to his fellow Roman Soldiers and would they understand? Can he talk with his childhood friends whom he has not seen in a while? Or tell it to his mother Rubella, who is now at the rightful age of 65.

Julius and his mother go for a walk as he reminisces to her about the events that took place in Bethlehem many years ago that is causing him to rethink his life today. *(Our past should and do not define our future).* After taking a trip down memory lane, Julius and his mother both make the decision to convert to Christianity, today on this Sunday.

-

ACT I SCENE I
HOW CAN THIS BE

NARRATOR: *(Lights up. Music playing as Julius is walking up the aisle in full dress, Roman Soldier Uniform. His head is hanging down in sadness.)*

1. Keep Making Me by Sidewalk Prophets) Today is Friday and a Roman Soldier is walking the streets of Rome after yet another Crucifixion. He is broken and downhearted. You see, he is reminded of a crucifixion that took place many years ago, one in which he had played a major role. He is also reminded of a birth that happened one night while he was visiting his childhood friends in the hills of Jerusalem. How can he explain what happened to him in those hills many years ago when he was just a boy visiting his childhood friends? Can he tell his mother, Rubella? Can he tell one of the Soldiers? Or can he tell us his story? *(A living room setting is at the downstage. A young man enters from upstage right wearing a Roman soldier's uniform. He enters the room and tosses his helmet on the sofa. From stage right we hear a woman's voice calling the soldier's name.)*

RUBELLA: *(Off stage)* Julius, Julius is that you? *(Enters: on stage call again)* Julius, hi there, my son.

JULIUS: *(Lights up. Julius is sitting on the sofa with his head in his right hand and helmet on the sofa. He slowly raises his head as his mother enters)* Hello Mother. I am so very tired.

RUBELLA: *(Walking over to Julius on the sofa)* I thought I heard you come in, but I was not expecting you until Sunday evening.

JULIUS: *(Getting up to greet his mother)* I know, but we got a three day pass this time. *(Walks over to the window. Sounds of children playing are heard.)*

RUBELLA: Good, I am happy to see you. We can spend a little time together and talk before--- Julius I went---

JULIUS: Yes, mother, I was told that you were out and about incredibly early this morning before the sun was up. And on top of that you were alone!

RUBELLA *:(Interrupted)* I had to-----

JULIUS: *(Interrupted, turning away from the window to look at Mother)* During this time of year, Mother, you cannot go out early in the morning, especially alone!

RUBELLA: *(Taking a few steps to the sofa and picking up the helmet she looks at Julius and takes a seat in her chair)* I did not go alone. Julius Tobit was walking behind me. Besides, I had to pay my taxes, your father is dead, you were gone, and David is just too young to go alone to pay taxes.

JULIUS: *(Looking at his mother).* Mother, during this time of year, crucifixion, it is not safe for you to be walking around. Rocks are flying all over the place and you could be killed by one of them.

RUBELLA: *(Still seated)* I understand son, but you leave early in the morning before the sun comes up. And really, Julius I have to----

JULIUS: I am a Roman Soldier Mother, and I am trained to protect myself from danger. The Roman Army did teach me that much, *(lowered his voice)* but not how to love and care for another human being. I must leave early in the morning during crucifixion time. I need to be there to oversee the others and get ready for the crucifixion.

RUBELLA: *(Changing the subject, she walks back towards the kitchen)* Today is Friday and the day of crucifixion, any reason why the crowd was unusually heavy? I saw a multitude of people going up toward the hill. *(Stopped midway - turned and looked at Julius)* This reminded me of a few years ago when the people from Bethlehem came to the crucifixion of a man called Jesus and people from all over were there crying and screaming, crucify Him! Calling him Jesus, the Messiah, and saying He was the King of the Jews. How could that be? We only have one king and that is Ce----

JULIUS: *(Still looking out the window)* Say what Mother?

RUBELLA: *(Walks up to Julius and places her hand on his back)* Son? What is going on? What is on your mind? You have not been yourself since you got home.

JULIUS: Not much, just watching the boys and their friends playing with the lamb. *(Turned away from the window to look at his mother)* It reminds me of my friends and me playing with Solo the lamb in this same place. *(Sounds of children playing and of a lamb's bleat).*

RUBELLA: *(Laughing and walking back towards the kitchen but stops)* Yes, I recall how much you enjoyed playing with your friends. But I also recall that there were occasions when you would spend time alone in those hills. Your father would always say, "That boy is going to be a shepherd like most of the men in this family". Of course, I would always say to your father that you will become a philosopher, a writer, or even a teacher or someone great and well known by everyone.

JULIUS: Oh yea, I remember spending hours and hours playing with my friends in those Hills. *(laughter)* We heard a lot of great tales about Shepherds and sheep from our fathers. Those were good times. *(Take a seat on the sofa)* Maybe, I should have become a shepherd. Life sure would have been a lot simpler. And the only blood on my hands would be that of an animal and not that of a man, such as this man they call JESUS. *(Julius remains seated with his head in his hands; while music is playing.)*

RUBELLA: *(Grabs both of Julius' hands)* Son would you like to tell me what is on your mind?

JULIUS: Well Yes, sure why not it might just make me feel better *(throws both hands in the air)* and I can make some sense of what is going on in my head. I just do not know where to start.

RUBELLA: *(Going over to a corner in the room and getting her wrap and walking stick)* Come Julius let us go for a walk and you can start at the beginning. That is always a good place to start.

JULIUS: *(Walking on the line and picking up his helmet both Julius and his mother exits stage left)* Well, mother you see it all started to happen one night in Bethlehem when I---- *(Lights fade out as Julius begins to talk, but need to complete statement)*

2. SOFT MUSIC (musician's choice)

ACT I SCENE II
A YOUNG GIRL WITH A MYSTERIOUS MESSAGE

NARRATOR: Julius goes to visit his friends. They are now teenagers who are shepherd boys in the hills of Jerusalem watching their sheep when suddenly, a snoring sound is heard from behind a cluster of rocks and a messenger appears with wonderful news. "...**Waiting for the Right Moment...**" (*Joseph 16, Benjamin 16, Julius 15 and Reuben 15 are all teenagers, except for David 11 and Peter 10. As the curtain opens, Julius and Rueben are DC talking and laughing. David and Peter are sitting on the ground playing with Solo the Lamb DL when suddenly the sound of snoring is heard coming from a rock cluster at upstage right*).

REUBEN: (*Walking up to Julius*) The boys sure would be happy to see you again Julius, it has been a while since your last visit.

DAVID & PETER: (*Still sitting on the ground - looks up and waves*) Hello there Julius.

DAVID: Yes, Julius where have you been keeping yourself? Dancing the night away in Jerusalem? (*Both boys laugh while getting up*)

PETER: Yea where? (B*oth boys run off R*)

JULIUS: (*Carrying a duffle bag over his left shoulder*) I know my father and mother have been so remarkably busy with all those festivals. Boy am I so glad they are over for a while, at least until next spring anyway. They can get a little loud and out of control sometimes. (*Both boys stumble, as if drunk*).

REUBEN: (*Laughing*) I heard it can last for days.

MESSENGER: (S*noring from behind the rocks and pausing after each snore*) Snore, snore, snore.

JULIUS: (L*ooking around as if searching for something*) Did you hear that?

REUBEN: Did I hear the what?

MESSENGER: (Snores a little louder) **Snore, snore, snore**...

JULIUS: That!? There it goes again. That sound.

REUBEN: No Julius, I did not. Your ears are still ringing from all that loudness and music from the festivals. (Pulling Julius's ear) It is so quiet in these hills one can hear a cotton drop.

JULIUS: I will say it is always quiet around here and: therefore, the least amount of a different sound can be heard if you are not talking and making jokes.

REUBEN: Yes, I guess so, anyway I like the quietness. It gives me time to think.

JULIUS: Wow! THINK, did you say THINK, wow! Here I was only thinking you speak without thinking. I did not know you could think. (*Laughs and tags Reuben in a boyish playful way*). By the way, where are Peter and David?

REUBEN: (*Pointing off R*) probably over that ridge with the others and playing with Solo the lamb.

MESSENGER: (*Snoring is a lot louder now. Peeping over the rocks and trying to get the boys' attention. As Julius and Reuben turns toward the rocks, the messenger slips down trying to avoid the boys from seeing her*). Snore, snore, snore… (*Pausing for four seconds after each snore*)

JULIUS: Ok, there it goes again. You must have heard it that time.

REUBEN: Yes, I heard it that time. (*Pointing in the direction of the rocks. Julius puts down his bag and the boys tiptoes toward the rocks over at downstage left. Julius picks up a small stone and tosses it in the direction of the cluster*).

MESSENGER: (*Getting up and rubbing the top of her head*) OUCH!! What you did that for? Who threw that stone at me? Don't you know you should not throw stones around here? You might hit something or someone, like me!

REUBEN: Who are you and what are you doing in these hills?

JULIUS: Girls always want to be where they should not be. Who are you and what are you doing here?

REUBEN: Are you all right?

MESSENGER: Who me? Yes, I am, sure, I think so. My head is just a little sore after you hit me with that stone.

REUBEN: Sorry, if you are hurt, I will be happy to---

MESSENGER: (*Walking on the line and going off Left*) Oh, that is ok. I am alright.

JULIUS: What are you doing here in these hills anyway?

REUBEN: Julius.

MESSENGER: Just waiting. (*Walking on line exiting L*)

BOTH BOYS: Waiting for what, who, when? (*Looking at each other and laughs*)

JULIUS: (*Cuffs mouth and yells*) Well, we are waiting for an answer!

MESSENGER: (Off stage) For the right moment.

BOTH BOYS: (*Looking at each other in confusion*) The right moment?

JULIUS: She is talking a little strange if you ask me.

REUBEN: She sure is. Maybe that stone you threw might have done something to her head.

JULIUS: I do not understand what moment she is talking about.

MESSENGER: (*Off L*) You will in time, Julius.

REUBEN: Wait a minute, hold up, I will walk with you. Hold… (*Moving closer L, but stops and looks at Julius*)

JULIUS: I do not think she heard you man. And how does she know my name?

REUBEN: She heard me. I do not know how she knows your name, but maybe she was at one of those festivals your parents held. You know how girls are. They like to have it their way. (*Yells out*) Wait up! Girls should not be walking in these hills alone! A little bump on the head and a giant sized headache she is. (*Both boys laugh*)

JULIUS: Thanks Reuben that sure makes me feel a lot better knowing that I might have really hurt her.

REUBEN: I hope not! She is fine. Maybe we should have gone with her and walked her out of the hills. (*Looking over for David and Peter*) Where did David and Peter go?

JULIUS: (*Picking up bag*) Well, I am going to find Joseph and Benjamin. David and Peter must be with them.

REUBEN: You sure you want to go looking for them alone? Hey, by the way, can you stay over tonight?

JULIUS: (*Walking on line from L to exit R*) Yes, I can. It took a lot of begging my parents, and I even got down on my knees. (*Rubbing his knees*) My knees are still sore from all that begging (*laughing while going off at UR*)

REUBEN: (*Sitting on the ground playing with the small stones and talking to himself*) That boy is going to make a good shepherd one day. Nah~~h, I think he would become a Roman Soldier like his uncle.

3. I AM NOT ALONE *by Natalie Grant---CC* *(Curtain close)*

ACT II SCENE I
THE WEARY SERVANTS SIT DOWN

NARRATOR: A man's work is not measured by his success. Rather he is measured by the faithfulness to the task by which he is called. As the Messiah was about to enter the world, God was on the move not only to declare defeat over sin but to provide joy and gladness to the righteous. God upsets the atmosphere to tragedy and pain, to prepare the way for the Good News. God wanted to remind the faithful that in His Kingdom and under Christ's reign there is something far more superior than the pain and suffering that we will most certainly walk through in this life. The boys are about to walk through a bit of pain with the loss of a lamb called Solo.

REUBEN: *(Lights up- Reuben tossing small stones and talking to himself. A lamb is crying as Reuben tosses another stone).* Ba~~ba~~~ba~~. All right, all right I am coming, ba~~ba~~ba~~. I hear you. Keep your lamb's wool on. (H*umming as he is walking towards the lamb)* Here I am. Your shepherd is here now. *(Sitting on the rocks and taking the lamb in his arms and looking up at the sky, he places index finger and thumb rubbing chin as if thinking)* I wonder if King David ever got bored when he was a shepherd boy?... Nope, I do not think he did. Of course he could sing, and he had a harp to keep his company. Of course, I could sing, but I just might cause a sheep stamped *(Reuben begins to sing and dance while holding lamb)*

4. I WILL SING LIKE DAVID SANG

BENJAMIN: Reuben! Reuben! *(While Reuben is still singing Benjamin is calling Reuben's name. Benjamin enters still calling and out of breath)* Reuben! O' there you are.

REUBEN: *(Getting up as Benjamin approaches him)* Hey Benjamin, you looking for me? Well, here I am - me and my sheep. Did Julius find you? And Joseph, he went looking for you too. By the way, are Peter and David with you?

BENJAMIN: They are coming. *(Still out of breath)*

JOSEPH: *(Enters from DR and out of breath, coughing and wheezing, stops halfway, leans on his staff)* I am coming, I am coming. *(Entering stage half out of breath)* Getting too old for this. Climbing these hills are going to be the death of me before I am----- well let us just say before I am my father's age.

BENJAMIN: Sure Joseph, now where are the others?

JOSEPH: If they have any sense, they would have stopped to rest as I should have. Sorry, we are late Reuben.

REUBEN: That's ok Joseph. *(Taps Benjamin on the shoulder and whispers)* Joseph makes being late a career. *(Walks over to Joseph and helps on stage)* Hey Joseph, it is so nice to see that you are once again in good health with no complaints.

JOSEPH: (*Moving closer to the rocks*) That is not funny, Reuben, I am on my last leg and you are making jokes. I have got to sit down for a minute or two.

REUBEN: Here, sit down on this rock, Joseph, for as long as you want. *(Pointing to the big rock)*

BENJAMIN: It will sure feel good to sit down again. Okay now about you Reuben, what is going on with you?

JOSEPH: My feet are killing me, and nobody cares. Some friends you are. (*Leaning on his staff and moving closer to another cluster of rocks while laughing Benjamin and Reuben begins to sing*)

5. SIT DOWN SERVANT

BOTH BOYS-- Sit down Servant sit down, sit down and rest a little while. *(They all laugh)*

REUBEN: *(Getting up)* Here let me help you Joseph *(Grabbing Joseph's arm and leading him to the other clutter of rocks)*

BENJAMIN: *(Sitting on the rock next to Reuben he whispers to Ruben in a joking way)* His back hurts; his neck is sore and his—

REUBEN: *(Interrupts)* and his hearing is not so good either.

JOSEPH: I heard that. You are talking about me and I am right here my friends??

BENJAMIN: And by the way, he did not sleep too well last light.

REUBEN: Oh why? *(Before Benjamin could answer, Reuben changes the subject)* Hey did you see a girl walking in these hills on your way here?

BENJAMIN: No Reuben, and besides no girl, woman, or any female of any kind would be walking alone in these hills.

REUBEN: She did, I assure you. She was a young girl around our age with dark hair, glowing smooth skin, and very pretty. Julius and I heard snoring coming from behind these rocks and Julius threw a small stone and hit her in the head. Then she started talking funny. We asked her why she was here in these hills. She said she was waiting for the "**right moment**", and that I, we would know when the right time comes. I do not know what that means. Do you Benjamin? We-

JOSEPH: *(Interrupts Reuben)* Sure Reuben; sun got to you. No female ever comes up in these hills especially a pretty young girl with dark hair and glowing smooth skin.

BENJAMIN: *(Looking at Joseph)* Let him finish, Joseph. Sounds like he has a story to tell.
REUBEN: Here comes Julius. He can tell you that we both saw this girl and what she said.

JULIUS: *(Running on stage and out of breath)* Reuben, Reuben! Solo the lamb is missing! I went down to the river to get the boys and get a drink of water and I saw them playing a game called "seek and find me". Then I heard Peter yelling for Solo and crying to David that he couldn't find his lamb. I thought it was a part of the game when David started yelling the lamb's name. *(Out of breath)* I ran back up the bank and saw that Solo was really missing! I joined in the search, but he is nowhere to be found! Reuben, He is missing! We cannot find him!

BENJAMIN: I am sure the boys are just playing a joke on you Julius, as they do with us, too.

JOSEPH: I am sure when we get back there, Solo will be in David's arms.

JULIUS: No! It is not a joke Benjamin. I am telling you Solo is lost! I do not know where he is, we looked for him everywhere. *(Turns to look at Joseph. He had already begun walking to help in the search for the lamb. (Lights fade out as Benjamin and Reuben start walking off UL. CC (curtain close- lights down when the last person exited stage)*

ACT II SCENE II
A LOST LAMB IS FOUND

NARRATOR: 6. SOFT MUSIC PLAYING. Luke 15: 4-6. "Suppose one of you has a hundred sheep and loses one of them. Doesn't he leave the 99 in the open country and go after the lost sheep until he finds it? And when he finds it, he joyfully puts it on his shoulders and goes home. Then he calls his friends and neighbors together and says, rejoice with me; I have found my lost sheep." The boys are now young adults. It has been many years since they have been in these hills together. Now here they are once again sitting around a campfire eating cheese and bread talking about what happened earlier when Solo the Lamb went missing and strange things begin to happen. (*Young Julius, Reuben, and Joseph are sitting around a campfire talking, and eating cheese & bread. David and Peter come in walking behind adult Julius and his mother. David and Peter take their seat around the other boys. Adult Julius is still telling his mother about that day. They are walking toward the stage from the floor going up steps to stage halfway. The lights come up on stage, music stops playing, adult Julius begins speaking*).

Adult JULIUS: *(Enter DL)* You see Mother, after we went looking for Solo that night, things began to happen, and changes came about. (*Exit L*)

REUBEN: *(The boys are laughing. Once adult Julius and his mother exits, Reuben begins to speak)* Boy, we looked everywhere for Solo that evening.

JOSEPH: For sure those little four-legged creatures, can surely give you a giant size scare sometimes.

Y.A. JULIUS: I was afraid of some wild animal or something coming out from these hills and getting to him before we did.

BENJAMIN: (*Entering from 'DR' carrying his staff*) Hey boys, any food left? I am starving!

JOSEPH: Yes, we do, but first give us a report and please no bad news this time. My heart cannot take it again. *(Jokingly)* I am not a well man you know.

REUBEN: *(Shaking his head)* Yeah right, you are always saying that Joseph. You certainly did not let poor health stop you from helping us search for the Lamb that afternoon. I never saw anyone move so fast that is in such bad health as you claim to be in. *(Laughter)*

JOSEPH: Well, He was an incredibly special little Lamb.

BENJAMIN: Things are simply fine around and all is well and quiet. As a matter of fact, the thing is it's unusually quiet in these hills tonight. The sheep are not even talking tonight *(sitting on the ground next to the campfire)*. Enough about Solo the Lamb and the small talk. Now, can I have some food?

REUBEN: *(Breaking a piece of bread and cheese - handed it to Benjamin)* Eat up my man, eat up.

BENJAMIN: *(Turning the bread, overlooking at the ridiculously small pieces)* Sure, you can spare it my friend? *(Everybody laughs)*

JULIUS: Give the man a bigger piece of bread and some more cheese to go with it. He surely worked for it 10 years ago. Besides, he is a growing man. (*Making a round belly shape with his hand. All laughs*)

REUBEN: Benjamin, we were just talking about that day when Solo the Lamb went missing. I remember you being the first one on the scene. Come to think of it, weren't you the one who found him?

BENJAMIN: No, it was Joseph who was the hero. By the way, Joseph, that was nice work for an OLD shepherd in POOR health.

JULIUS: Joseph, tell us how you found Solo.

JOSEPH: Nothing to it *(Cuffing left ear while looking out in the audience)* I just listened for a minute, then I heard a faint lamb crying for help, so I ran toward the edge of the cliff where the sound was coming from and looked down. There he was. I jumped in and pulled him out. Peter and David loved that lamb so very much. I just had to do all I could to get him back for them. Besides, he was a lost lamb crying out for his shepherd.

BENJAMIN: Well, you saved the life of a small lamb and got him to his shepherd. Good for you my man, good for you.

JOSEPH: *(DRC standing at attention. Puffed out his chest)* All in a day's work my boys, all in a day's work.

JULIUS: I never could understand what is so special about Solo the Lamb. He is just a lamb, the same as any one of them around here.

REUBEN: Yes, he is just a lamb, but a good shepherd never leaves his sheep behind. My father always said a good shepherd protects and take care of his sheep at all time. *(CC. lights down)*

ACT III SCENE I
THE JOURNEY TO BETHLEHEM

NARRATOR 1: 7. ABABY CHANGES EVERYTHING *by Faith Hill (Spotlights on narrators)* It was in God's plans for Joseph to take Mary to Bethlehem where His Son Jesus Christ was to be born. Joseph had to take Mary to his hometown, Bethlehem. It was no coincidence that Caesar issued his decree at that time. A prophecy written down some seven centuries earlier foretold that the Messiah would be born in Bethlehem. Now, it so happened that there was a town named Bethlehem a mere seven miles from Nazareth. However, the prophecy specified that it was Bethlehem Ephrathah that would produce the Messiah. (Micah 5:2) They did not have cars in those days, so it took them anywhere from five to seven days to journey to that little village from Nazareth to Bethlehem. Covering some eighty hilly miles and walking over rocks, dirt roads, and dealing with the early mid-autumn weather of light rains and the end of the dry season. Come to think of it that is the same distance between Beaufort and North Charleston. This journey was very tiding for Mary since she was soon to give birth.

NARRATOR 2: They stopped at many motels along the way trying to get a room for the night, but there was just NO ROOM in the Inns. Arriving at Joseph's ancestral home, they found it already full of other family members who had arrived earlier. Once again there was NO ROOM in the Guest House on the second floor for Mary and Joseph. The Innkeeper took them to another part of the house where a small number of flock animals were housed inside on the ground floor room. This is where animals, tools, and agricultural produce were stored, food was prepared and consumed. You see, by animals being inside, the animals were protected from theft and the elements of the weather, also with them being inside they provided body heat for cool nights, milk and fuel or substitute for firewood (Luke 13:8.) Joseph and Mary did not find room in the living quarters of the ancestral family home. Instead, they stayed downstairs in the domestic stable, but still within the keeping of the family home where a manger or two were kept. Here is where the angels, shepherds, and maybe the wise men visited the baby Jesus. The book of Matthew tells us that Jesus' life began in a stable, a small barn where animals were kept. Doesn't it seem strange that our Lord, the King of kings, the King of the Jews, the Messiah, The Alpha and Omega was not born in a fancy palace or even on the main floor of the guest house? Well, this was God's plan and look at what the outcome is. We now have a chance of a life that is full of the hope of living with that Baby Boy we call Jesus the Messiah, the One and only. That night was the most exciting and wonderful night the world had ever witnessed.

JOSEPH: 8. NO ROOM IN THE INN *by Shawna Edward (Singing as walking up the aisle after traveling awhile in the hot sun and mostly on foot. Joseph looked at Mary, he saw that she was looking weak so he went up to the nearest Inn, knocked on the door of an Inn, asked the Innkeeper for a room who pointed to the sign in bold red letters, after saying a few choice words)* Mary do you want to rest a while? There is an Inn. I will go see if there is any room.

MARY: Yes Joseph, I would, I am a little hot and a lot tired.

JOSEPH: *(Joseph knocking on the hotel office door not noticing the sign in all caps and bold red letters that read FULL NO ROOM a man enters from 'DR' dressed in his robe and a nightcap, half-asleep adjusting his clothes)* Sir, do you have a room for me and my__

INN KEEPER#1: (*Before Joseph could finish his statement the Inn Keeper interrupted*). Didn't you see the sign!? Can't you read!? (*Pointing to the sign above the door*) it reads **FULL NO ROOM** in **BOLD RED** letters even! (*Turning away from Joseph, the innkeeper slams and locks the door while still talking to himself in anger*) Can you people from Nazareth read! NO! I guess not "What good can come out of Nazareth!?" How many times must I get up just to say FULL NO ROOM! (*Innkeeper's wife walks up to him adjusting her robe*) Go back to sleep my Dear. Just another Nazareth who **cannot** read! (*Exit R yarning*)

JOSEPH: Thank you sir. (*Walking back to where Mary is, he has a sad look in his eyes as he brings himself to tell her there is No Room in the Inn, as he is helping Mary up from the rock singing*) Come on Mary, there is no room, maybe the next Inn would have a place for us to stay for the night. We must find a place for you to rest very soon.

MARY: (*Getting up holding her stomach*) I truly hope so Joseph, because I do not think this boy is going to wait much longer. He is surely ready to come into this world (*They both laugh and continued their journey. 'DL' Once in Bethlehem, Joseph and Mary stopped at another Inn which just happened to be his family's, Guest House Inn. Joseph walks up to the door and knocks without taking notice of yet another sign that read NO ROOM.*

INNKEEPER: (*Innkeeper opens door and saw that it was Joseph, welcomes him in and took one look at Mary then throws up his hands after talking to Joseph.*) Sorry Joseph, there is no room on the second floor of the Guest House, but I can make room for you and Mary on the first floor where we keep the animals and produces.

JOSEPH: (*Joseph being thankful for a place for Mary to rest, he grabbed her hand and helped her into the house*) Thank you, good man. She is very tired after such a long journey. The 1st floor where you keep the animals will be simply fine. (*Inn Keeper, Joseph and Mary exits L. Lights down*)

9. WE SHALL BEHOLD HIM *by Sandi Patty* **(dance ministry)**

ACT III SCENE II
O' HOLY NIGHT

NARRATOR: (*Video of the birth of Jesus may be shown while the narrator is speaking*) Yes, that was an extremely exciting and wonderful night. Mary gave birth to a Baby Boy. Not just any baby boy, just like the angel told them back in Nazareth. "You shall give birth to a Baby Boy and you shall call Him Jesus. He will be great and will be called the Son of the Most High. Like most babies, the Baby Jesus fell asleep in his mother's arm and she wrapped Him in a white cloth. The Innkeeper's wife along with the other women guests made room for the baby to lay in an animal feeding box with hay and cloths, one of which was white linen. Mary laid Him there to rest as she and Joseph looked on just like today's parents do when their newborn falls asleep for the first time. I read in a child's storybook that even the animals somehow knew that this baby was not just any baby, because they too made room for His entrance to this world. I read that the Doves ko-o-ed, the cows mooed, the lamb ba-a- as, and the donkey bucked, kicking over a feeding box in excitement. A star with a long and brighter tail than any other star ever seen could be seen for miles around. Matthew 2 tells us that kings, wise men, and shepherds saw the star and rejoiced with exceeding great joy. They came from miles to seek the child and when they saw the baby, they fell to their knees to worship Him. How great that was then and how great it is still today Oh, what an *O'HOLY NIGHT that was!*

JOSEPH: (*Curtain opens, lights up. Boys still sitting around a campfire when suddenly Joseph covers his eyes for a few seconds then opens them and points to the star in the East) looking at his friends*) I have never seen one like it before!

BENJAMIN: (*Blocking his eyes from the bright light, looking up to where Joseph is pointing*) You are right Joseph, it is very bright. I have never seen one so bright.

JULIUS: (*Still sitting and not looking at the star in a nonchalant matter of fact way*) I noticed it earlier. It did not seem important to me. Besides, what does it mean? (*Boys look at him*)

REUBEN: It looks like it is standing still over something. Wait a minute; it is in the direction of Bethlehem of Galilee. The tail looks like a pointer.

JULIUS: (*Still sitting on the ground*) My father will know what it means. I will ask him when I see him. He knows about these such things.

(*Soft Music 10. RISE UP SHEPHERD) Angels enter from stage left: the boys do not see the angel standing in a distant*)

JOSEPH: (*Putting the bread back in a sack*) More bread anyone?

JULIUS: No thank you, Joseph, I am stuffed. (*Rubbing his belly*)

BENJAMIN: Sure, why not. I am hungry. (*Reaching for the cheese and bread*)

ALL: You are always hungry Benjamin! (*Boys laugh*)

JOSEPH: I am a bit chilly. You know, I remember the same chill came over me that night many years ago. Strange things happened that night when Solo was lost. Colder than ever, oh yes, a bright star. Yes, that bright Star. What else happened—? *(As Joseph is getting up, he notices the angels standing afar; his mouth opens, drops his staff and falls to his knees)*

BENJAMIN: Joseph! *(Soon as he called out Joseph's name, he too sees the angels. The other boys turn around to see what happened. At that moment they too see the angels and fall to their knees except for Julius)*

[Young] **JULIUS: (***Running over to help Benjamin and Joseph up and away from the angel. He suddenly feels weak and falls face down with both arms stretch out)* Benjamin! Joseph. *(Offstage adult Julius talking to his mother)* Mother that night so much happened to me. It did not seem real. The angels began to speak after I fell. *(Angels enter from DLS with angel #3 in front, followed by 2 and 4, 1 and 5 in back)*

ANGEL 3: *(Dressed in bright blue)* Do not be afraid, I bring you good news.

ANGELS 2& 4*: (Dressed in blue)* News of great joy.

ANGEL 1: *(Dressed in white, moving closer to the boys)* "Fear not: for behold I bring you good tidings of great joy, which shall be to all people. For unto you is born this day in the city of David a Savior, which is Christ the Lord. And this shall be a sign unto you; ye shall find the babe wrapped in swaddling clothes, lying in a manager".

ANGEL 5: (W*alks over to Joseph and lightly touches him)* Rise, follow the star East to Bethlehem of Judea and there you shall bow down to Him, the Messiah, whom you waited for. *(The boys begin to get up looking at each other and back at the angels as the angels exit R The child David and Peter enters L, one boy singing and the other tapping the drum exit L).*

11. THE LITTLE DRUMMER BOY.

PETER: *(After child finish singing)* Why didn't you say something Benjamin?

JOSEPH: Did you see what was happening Peter? Did you hear all those voices? Like I said, strange things were happening that night?

BENJAMIN: Say something Peter? There was nothing for me to say! Besides, I tried to open my mouth and speak but my mouth would just not open. I have never seen or heard anything like it in my life. And being a shepherd, you see and hear a lot in these hills.

DAVID: It was a dream and each of us were having the same dream at the same time with our eyes wide opened. *(Giggling)*

JULIUS: It really did not happen guys, like David said it was a dream with our eyes opened and we all were having the same dream at the same time. I still cannot wrap my mind around it.

BENJAMIN: Only thing is it did happen. Remember what the angels said? Good news for all mankind. After waiting for so many years, our Savior came. Just like our fathers and their fathers before them had been saying

JOSEPH: *(Standing and looking out at audience lift hands in praise)* **Praise God in the Highest!!!**

REUBEN: *(Yelled out)* The God of our ancestors, Abraham, and Jacob, the True and Living God!

JULIUS: *(Getting up from the ground he speaks to each boy while touching them on the shoulder in a demanding voice)(To Joseph)*What I don't understand is the angles said that night that He was a baby! *(To Benjamin)* How can a baby save all mankind!? *(To Reuben)* Your God is a baby? *(To Peter)*You worship a child, a baby!? *(To David)* How can this be!? *(Looking out to the audience after sitting down)*A baby has **No** powers! How can this be!?

JOSEPH: *(In a soft calm voice)*Yes, Julius, that is what the angles said alright, "A Babe is born, the Savior and He shall save all mankind."See Julius, that baby was born into royalty and was not just any baby, but He came to be the Savior of the world. He was born, He became a man, He died for our sins, He was buried, and He was resurrected that you and I may have everlasting life.

DAVID: Ok not to change the subject, but man it seemed like it took us a year to walk to Bethlehem of Galilee to see the baby, and when we finally got there, there he was in a manger with his mother watching over him wrapped in white linen clothing.

REUBEN: There were Wise Men from many countries that gave him expensive gifts. We honored His birth with a…

DAVID: I know right! We honored His birth with a lamb! That was the best gift of all! He smiled at me for it, too. Of course, the lamb was all we had to give you know. I think I was saved that night. I became a changed person, thinking differently, talking differently, and of course, loving even Julius more than ever *(Hugs Julius - all laugh. CC lights down)*

ACT IV SCENE I
THAT WAS THEN THIS IS NOW

NARRATOR: Music12. THAT WAS THEN, THIS IS NOW *by Josh Wilson.* Who you were, in the beginning, should not be who you are in the present. "The secret of change is to focus all of your energy not on fighting the old, but on building the new" *(a quote from a character named Socrates by Dan Millman)* Julius' life is about to make a "U" turn. Some years ago, Julius's life was a mess and he felt something was missing. The passion for life that his childhood friends had, he did not share it with them. After many days, weeks, months, years, and yes even crucifixions, it still took him a long time to trust he could make the right decision. He had been so convinced that the earlier decision that his family and the Roman nation had made to serve and worship their king was the right one. You see Julius' heart was no longer in it, and the passion he knew had gone. But, now Julius is convinced that it is time for him to make the "U" turn". Julius' decision to take the road less traveled from the road of destruction felt like absolutely the right thing to do and started a relationship with the BABY born in the lower room of the guest house where the animals were kept in Bethlehem. We changed and evolved. Why shouldn't our choices and decisions? Is Julius going to make the right decision?

RUBELLA: *(Offstage)* Julius? Did you go with the boys that night? Is that why____?

JULIUS: *(Adult Julius off stage)* No mother, but something happened to me, too. I do not know what.

BENJAMIN: We could have given Him a sheep, a full-grown sheep, but no, Peter insisted that we give Him Solo the Lamb that was lost and found, the one He loved the most.

PETER: Of course, the Messiah must have the best; only, the best for the one who is to save mankind.

[YA] JULIUS: *(Scratches his head)* All of this is still confusing to me. It was ten years ago, and it is still confusing, even now. I keep trying to figure it out, even now.

REUBEN: Well, Julius like the messenger said that day in the hills. The one you hit in the head with that stone remembers. You will understand when the time comes. Well, here it is. *(Puts a hand on Julius's shoulder while shaking his head)*

BENJAMIN: What I do not understand Peter, is why you wanted to stay behind to watch the sheep?

PETER: Why not? Someone had to look after the flocks and like you always say, a good shepherd never leaves his sheep. Besides, I figured it was time I proved to everyone that I could be responsible.

JOSEPH, BENJAMIN, and REUBEN: *(Together)* And you proved it that night! *(Laughing)*

PETER: *(Serious tone in his voice)* I never told you guys this, *(getting to his feet and walking around in thoughts)* but that night a messenger appeared once again back behind those rocks *(points to clusters)*. She said it was nice of me to stay behind and watch the other sheep. She also said the baby born that night, we shall call him Jesus and many changes will come about for all generations. Well, while she was talking, I heard the sheep moving about or so what I thought was the sheep, turned out it was Julius. She kept on talking, there were some things she said that was not making much sense. I turned around to Julius, but when I turned around to get some input from Julius, he was running away. She said that things will begin to happen. At His 33rd birthday, daylight would begin turning to night, hail would come at the noon hour of the day, and there would be a soldier who would become a faithful follower. *(Once again in the middle of the conversation, Julius disappears)* Of his turning his life from evil to good and becoming free and forgiven for his sins… Julius, I always wondered why you ran. She said some amazing things. *(Julius did not answer why he had run away 'URC' again)*

13. HOW CAN THIS BE by Lauren Daigle *CC. slowly.*

FINAL ACT
THE CHANGE OF A LIFETIME

NARRATOR: 14. **HELP ME FIND IT** by *Sidewalk Prophets*. Can this be the time that Julius confesses to his mother and to himself the change he felt that night? Julius and Rubella, his mother, is back home now, and he is still reminiscing about what happened those many years ago when he and his friends were just boys. Julius finally has come to terms with what things the messenger and the angels had mentioned, which has now come to reality. This Soldier's life is changed forever. Let us eavesdrop on this final conversation Julius is having with his mother. *Lights up* and curtain opens slowly. *(Julius sitting in a chair and Rubella on the sofa talking and putting the final pieces together to the end of a great life journey of events)*

RUBELLA: Julius, you never told me or your father what happened that night.

JULIUS: That is because I thought of it as a dream and never wanted to believe any of it or that it ever happened.

RUBELLA: But why not son? You should not have kept this to yourself all these years.

JULIUS: I thought no one would believe me, especially father.

RUBELLA: For over 20 years you kept this secret? I do remember hearing talk about a virgin, a baby and his name shall be called Jesus, He is the King, but I only thought of it as gossip.

JULIUS: Why mother?! *(Jumped up from the sofa and walked to UC looking out at the audience)* ...because people around here say nothing good could ever come out of Nazareth? Or is it because He was said to be the KING! Savior of the world?!

RUBELLA: Why no son! It is just that----well---- *(servant walks in L and bow)*

TOBIT: *(Bow)* Excuse me, my lord, I was worried about your mother since I had not seen her for a while and heard she went for a walk. This time of year, it is dangerous on the streets of Jerusalem. I was only told that she went for a walk.

JULIUS: Thanks for your concern, Tobit, but she is alright. I was with her. We went for a long walk.

TOBIT*: (Bow)* Yes, my lord, I can see she is in good hands. Good evening. *(Backs out while bowing)*

JULIUS: *(Turns and look at mother walking on line DRC)* Well deep in my heart, I know that the man I helped get nailed to the cross, the man we crucified on that Friday, was that same Baby that was born that night in Bethlehem of Galilee!

RUBELLA: I thought those men crucified were all common criminals. I heard about a man named Jesus being crucified. Now what makes you think that he was one of the same or yet the baby born in Bethlehem of Galilee?

JULIUS: Well, mother for sure, He was different. He spoke with authority, and He said things that no other man would have said. He was not guilty of any criminal charges.

RUBELLA: I am not sure He was not guilty. He went around healing and doing things on the Sabbath and that was a crime. You know that!

JULIUS: I am not sure He was guilty of that mother.

RUBELLA: Then why was He crucified?

JULIUS: I do not know mother! I just do not know! Maybe, He was born to be crucified. *(Stumped his feet)* Why???

RUBELLA: Son, you still have not told me what happened last Friday. What happened today to make you think that the baby born in Bethlehem was the same man that was on the cross?

JULIUS*: (Grabbing his mother's hand and walks over to the sofa)* I heard the wonderful things he did. I saw a great number of people following Him; men, women and children, women with babies, blind men, and all kinds of sick people. Mother, even after giving Him vinegar to drink, He said things that made everyone stop and listen to Him. He even gave me a smile, while blood and water were running down His side and face. He till smiled at me. (*Restless and confused, Julius gets up from the sofa rubbing his forehead - takes a few steps back to the window, stops and stumps his foot)* With a voice of thunder, He looked up to the sky *(Julius looking up)* as if He was talking to someone and said "Father forgive them for they know not what they are doing!" *(Walked back to mother on the* sofa) Daylight became night, and it even started to hail in the middle of sunlight. It started to rain just before we took him off the cross. *(Moving DC)* I remember the messenger telling Reuben the day will come and we would know that it is He. I also heard an angel talking to Peter telling him that these things will happen and a soldier's *(hitting chest)* life will change for the good. *(Moving RC, stops and looks at mother)* Mother! Could she have been talking about me! The angel~~ that angel was talking about me! I am sure of it!! *(Julius grabs mother's hand)*

RUBELLA*: (Hand in hand with Julius)* Son what do you mean you?! I did hear the thunder and saw the rain, but it all seemed like another stormy day, only just a bit worse. What do you mean it is you she was talking about?!!

JULIUS: *(Let's go of mother's hand and walks over to "DLC)* Certainly, that was a righteous man. He is living here in my heart. The baby, That BABY born on that autumn night in Bethlehem was the same man that was on that cross. *(Looking at mother and moves to DC)* Do you feel Him? I am a changed man. Today is the beginning of the rest of my life. The baby is right here. He has helped me pursue a lifelong change and to become a believer in Him who was born Savior of all mankind. **Even me!!** *(Julius begins to sing softly - choir joins in)*

15. I AM CHANGE by Natalie Harris

RUBELLA: *(Hugs Julius and joins in singing)* Son, I feel a change. He is here in my heart. *(Puts hand over heart)* *(Curtain closed with Julius and Rubella hugging and praising God. Dancers come to floor dancing to same)*

CALL TO DISCIPLESHIP: 16. DO YOU HAVE ROOM by Shawna Edwards

STAGE RIGHT ↑ UPSTAGE ↑ STAGE LEFT

			UP LEFT
UP RIGHT STAGE	UP RIGHT CENTER STAGE	UP LEFT CENTER STAGE	LEFT STAGE
RIGHT STAGE	RIGHT CENTER STAGE	LEFT CENTER STAGE	LEFT STAGE
DOWN RIGHT STAGE	DOWN CENTER STAGE	DOWN LEFT CENTER	DOWN LEFT STAGE

↓ ↓

DOWNSTAGE

↓

Boys seating place around campfire

Rueben Benjamin Joseph Julius Peter David

CHARACTER	ACT I--HOW CAN THIS BE	CAST
NARRATOR		
ADULT JULIUS-49***	ROMAN SOLIDER	
RUBELLA-65***	JULIUS' MOTHER	
ACT II	MYSTERIOUS MESSGE	
NARRATOR		
REUBEN-teenager		
DAVID-12	Playing marble with Peter	
PETER-10	Holding lamb & playing Marble with David	
MESSENGER-teenager		
JULIUS-teenager		
ACT II	THE WEARVY SERVANTS SIT DOWN	
NARRATOR	music playing softly in background	
REUBEN	I will Dance Like David Danced	
BENJAMIN		
JOSEPH	Sit Down Servant	
ACT III	A LOST LAMB IS FOUND	
NARRATOR		
ADULT JULIUS	Walking up steps after walk with mother	
REUBEN		
JOSEPH		
BENJAMIN		
JULIUS		
ACT III	JOURNEY TO BETHLEHEM	
NARRATOR	CD playing softly while narrator is speaking	
JOSEPH	JESUS' EARTHLY FATHER	
MARY	JESUS' MOTHER	
JESUS	BABY JESUS	
INN KEEPER I	HOSTILE INN KEEPER	

INN KEEPER WIFE	HOSTILE INN KEEPER WIFE	
INN KEEPER II	JOSEPH family member	
INN KEEPER WIFE		
ACT III	**O' HOLY NIGHT**	
NATTATOR		
JOSEPH		
BENJAMIN		
JULIUS		
RUEBEN		
DAVID		
PETER		
ANGEL 1		
ANGEL 2		
AMGEL 3		
ANGEL 4		
ANGEL 5		
Young Peter	Sing Drummer Boy/carry Lamb around neck	CAST
Young David	Beating drum	
ACT IV	**THAT WAS THEN THIS IS NOW**	
NARRATOR		
RUBELLA***		
ADULT JULIUS***		
BENJAMIN		
PETER		
JULIUS		
REUBEN		
JOSEPH		
FINAL ACT	**THE CHANGE OF A LIFETIME**	
NARRATOR		
RUBELLA	MAIN CHARACTER	
JULIUS	MAIN CHARACTER	
TOBIT	SERVANT OF	

LIST OF SONGS and MUSIC IN ORDER OF APPEARANCE

TITLE OF SONG	ARTIST	ACT	SCENE
1.KEEP MAKING ME	SIDEWALK PROPHETS	I	I
2.SOFT MUSIC	MUSICIAN CHOICE	I	I
3.I AM NOT ALONE	NATALIE GRANT	I	II
4.SING LIKE DAVID SANG	REUBEN	II	I
5.SIT DOWN SERVANT	BENJAMIN & REUBEN	II	I
6.SOFT MUSIC	MUSICIAN CHOICE	II	II
7. A BABY CHANGES EVERYTHING	FAITH HALL	III	I

8. NO ROOM IN THE INN	SHAWNA EDWARDS	III	I
9. WE SHALL BEHOLD HIM	SANDI PATTY	III	I
10. RISE UP SHEPHERD	HYMNAL	III	II
11.THE LITTLE DRUMMER BOY	PETER& DAVID	III	II
12.THAT WAS THEN THIS IS NOW	JOSH WILSON	IV	I
13.HOW CAN THIS BE	LAUREN DAIGLE	IV	I
14. HELP ME FIND IT	SIDEWALK PROPHIETS	Final	Act
15. I AM CHANGE	NATALIE HARRIS	Final	Act
16.DO YOU HAVE ROOM	SHAWNA EDWARDS	Final	Act

I OWN **NO** RIGHTS TO THESE SONGS/ songs may be change to suit act/scene

PROPS NEEDED
MICS
SOUND TEAM
TECH TEAM
LOVE SEAT or SOFA
ROGK CLUSTER (LAGER ENOUGH TO HIDE MESSENGER)
SMALL ROCKS AROUND STAGE and FLOOR
WALKING STICK (for Rubella)
DUFFER BAG (for Julius)
LOAF OF BREAD (unsliced)
BAR OF CHEESE
10 SHEPHERD STAFF (4 children and 6 adults)
SOUND EFFECT OF LAMB)
YouTube or CHOIR
SOLDIER HELMET
ROMAN SOLDIER UNIFORM
PICTURE WINDOW
WHITE DRESS/ROBE FOR ANGEL (color optional)
LIGHT BLUE ROBE /DRESS FOR MESSENER (color optional)
STUFFED LAMB
BACK DROPS
FEEDING BOX

Stage props needed by Acts:

Act 1
Roman Living Room Setting
Mother: Apron, wooden spoon, walking stick and shoulder wrap.
Solider: Helmet, Roman solider uniform.

Act 2 Scene 1
Rock Cluster, Hill scene backdrop with sheep, rocks on stage and floor, rock wrap, duffer bag, 2-3 stuffed sheep and lamb sound effect, rock for shepherd to sit on (2)

Act 2 Scene 2
Same as scene 1

Act 3 Scene 1 same as Act 2
Bread & Cheese
Campfire

Act 3 Scene 2: Two Red NO ROOM signs, Bethlehem Backdrop at stage left, Jerusalem, backdrop at stage right, props for Mary; Pull cart for, pregnant belly, white dress blue head dress. Joseph: brown/ Multicolor Robe and Cap, Staff.